FEISTYPets

GET FEISTY!

MAKE YOUR OWN RULES—THEN BREAK THEM

BY
SAMANTHA
GARLAND

SCHOLASTIC INC.

Photo credits: cover background pixels ©
The7Dew/Shutterstock; cover rip © AVS-Images/
Shutterstock; texture page 3 and throughout ©
A-Star/Shutterstock; bats page 54 © FabrikaSimf/
Shutterstock; ornaments page 57 © Nata-Lia/
Shutterstock.

ISBN 978-1-338-35861-2

10 9 8 7 6 5 4 3 2 1   19 20 21 22 23

Printed in the U.S.A.   40

First printing 2019

Book design by Mercedes Padró
and Kay Petronio

CONTENTS

wHeN SUGAR TURNS TO SPICE...

THEY'RE SOMETIMES NAUGHTY AND SOMETIMES NICE

THE FEISTY PETS

are one moody bunch. The gang may seem like lovable furry creatures, but watch out . . . their sweet smiles and doofy grins can turn to snarky snarls at any moment. Their adorable faces can lure in new friends with ease, but evidence shows the Feisty Pets are indeed mischievous troublemakers. This guide is the rule book they live by. Proceed with CAUTION!

THE FEISTY Pets™

GET TO KNOW THE **FEISTY** GANG

SAMMY SUCKERPUNCH

SAMMY likes to think of himself as one of the leaders of the Feisty Pets crew, but don't let that fool you—he still curls up in the laundry chewing crayons like any cuddly pup. Sammy's passion in life is sniffing butts, and he isn't afraid to let the world know.

PRINCESS POTTYMOUTH

On the outside, this kitty is sweet and pretty, but when she opens her mouth, her wicked grin says it all. She sleeps in on Sundays, and starts pulling pranks on Mondays. Watch out when **PRINCESS POTTYMOUTH** is on the prowl, and don't get in between her and anything sweet—her favorite food groups are sugar and preservatives!

SIR GROWLS-A-LOT

This fuzzy Pet is no cuddly teddy bear. After waking up from hibernating, **SIR GROWLS-A-LOT** is cranky and on the hunt for grub. There're rumors he's been arrested for breaking and entering restaurants to find raw steaks.

LIGHTNING BOLT LENNY

You might not guess it, but one of the most reckless and adventurous Feisty Pets is . . . a sloth. **LENNY** really hates being labeled "lazy," since he spends an average weekend cliff diving or drag racing. This tree-dweller doesn't need any caffeine—just the occasional nap . . . and a stress-free rom-com. And remember: Never mistake Lenny for a two-toed sloth.

GINORMOUS GRACIE

GiNorMous Gracie is tall. Like, really tall . . . 'cause she's a giraffe, duh. She shows off her long legs with cute leg warmers, but she's very self-conscious about her long neck. Never give her a scarf as a gift.

GRANDMASTER FUNK

GrandMaster FuNK is a sporty little monkey with a great arm. He can toss poo like no other. Catch him and Marky Mischief producing some sweet music collabs on your fave jungle jams. He also moonlights as a policeman on Feisty Films.

JACKED-UP JACKIE

JACKIE'S priority in life is her tiny joey, Kanga-Joey, but that doesn't mean she's not the feistiest mom out there. She kicks major kanga-butt at kickboxing and knows Liza Loca is jealous of her skills.

JUNKYARD JEFF

JEFF is a total goofball goat with a shouting habit. He'll tell you a hilarious knock-knock joke or give you unwanted advice . . . while screaming in your face. He also likes to talk about the "good ole days" with youngsters. At least he's a great motivator when you need him to be.

BLACK BELT BOBBY

Don't get on **BLACK BELT BOBBY'S** bad side. You'll come out with a black eye—this panda has a black belt, after all. On the other hand, he makes great desserts. Try his chocolate-covered bamboo if you're ever at his dinner parties.

LIZA LOCA

LIZA LOCA is a chatty koala bear who is always on the hunt for a good bargain. Stay away from her when she's texting, video-calling, tweeting, snapping, or 'gramming. Seriously, she'll bite.

LETHAL LENA

LeNA may be modest, but she's a freakin' Olympic athlete. She won the Feisty bobsledding silver medal in 2018! Just maybe don't hike on her mountain when she's practicing . . . people have been reported missing.

RASCAL RAMPAGE

RASCAL is a raccoon with a criminal past. He's been caught in his neighbors' pantries, stealing corn chips and junk food. He'll settle for trash if he gets kicked out, though, and always shares his stash with friends.

FREDDY WRECKINGBALL

FReDDy is known to trash-talk anyone who gets in his way, including Sammy Suckerpunch, his rival pup. He loves chewing bones and hates cats . . . and is actually feisty 90 percent of the time.

BILLY BLUBBERBUTT

BILLY BLUBBeRBuTT absolutely hates it when people think narwhals aren't real just because his horn is so gorgeous. It's unicorns that don't exist, not narwhals. As long as he gets the existence credit he deserves, he's actually a really cuddly Pet.

LADY MONSTERTRUCK

LADY MONSTERTRUCK is super emo. She paints her nails black every day, destroys living room furniture for fun, and takes pouty selfies with heavy black eyeliner.

FERDINAND FLAMEFART

FERDINAND is a totally romantic dragon. He and Sparkles Rainbowbarf are in a serious—though sometimes toxic—relationship. At parties, he loves to impress (or scare) everyone with his flames, and can always get the grill going and the s'mores gooey.

GLENDA GLITTERPOOP

GLeNDA thinks she is the glitziest Feisty Pet. Her superstar side is always on display in her vlogs, but not many know that she's a hidden nerd. Glenda is obsessed with zombie movies! She also enjoys experimenting with electrical sockets and studying the engineering behind them. Her makeup tutorials always end in disaster.

SPARKLES RAINBOWBARF

SPARKLeS loves to cruise around in fancy cars and show off her stylish wardrobe. She's a teensy bit spoiled and loooves getting presents or being treated like royalty, especially by her dragon boyfriend. Watch out for her rainbow tail.

RUDE ALF

R∪De ALF is one of Santa's reindeer . . . but he only helps when he feels like it. He's been known to sneak out for a joyride on Santa's sleigh with some of the other reindeer—and skydive right off into the snowflakes!

EBENEEZER CLAWS

Around Christmastime, EBeNeeZeR gets stuck helping out Santa at mall visits. He'll pose for pictures while kids plop on Santa's lap, flashing his feisty snarl. But when the adults have their backs turned, Ebeneezer steals holiday treats from unsuspecting children.

TAYLOR TRUELOVE

TAYLOR does NOT believe in cupid. She'd much rather listen to one of her multiple breakup song playlists. Her last feisty date ended with her throwing chocolates in her date's face when he admitted he didn't like Taylor Swift. She has an ongoing feud with Katy Cobweb.

KATY COBWEB

KATY enjoys playing spooky pranks in the middle of the night. October is obviously her favorite time of year, since she thinks it's flattering when people think she's bad luck. But she hates pumpkins, and will destroy any she sees. She used to be BFFs with Taylor Truelove.

CUDDLES VON RUMBLESTRUT

CUDDLES VON RUMBLESTRUT is from a fancy guinea pig family, yet he is known to be just as reckless as Lightning Bolt Lenny. In fact, the pair often teams up to push the limits of adventure and plan cliff-diving trips.

MARKY MISCHIEF

MARKY has many sides to his personality. He's an MC/king-of-the-jungle rapper who teams up with Grandmaster Funk to produce music, a pro wrestler, and a super-nerd who wears thick glasses and has a hard time getting a date. And he has trouble with his smartphone—Siri seems to like playing pranks on him.

VICKY VICIOUS

VICKY is full of RABBIT RAGE. And she lets it out with her passion for rap and rock music. She also spends the majority of her day at the Feisty Fit & Sweat Club lifting heavy weights. Wear closed toed shoes around this bunny . . .

KARL THE SNARL

KARL is all about the ice, ice, baby! He's a huge fan of all snowy sports and activities including hockey, ice-fishing, and polar bears vs. seals hunting games. If you see yellow snow, Karl was probably the culprit. He has always been obsessed with his looks, and loves taking selfies.

TONY is afraid of Karl. They've been too close for comfort on a number of group iceberg adventures. Tony's happy to eat his veggies and avoid fitness at all costs, but he'll base jump with the other seals occasionally.

SCARIN' ERIN

ERIN is a travel bug. She's especially fond of Paris; her gorgeous wings have reached the top of the Eiffel Tower many times! Once, on spring break, she even skydived from the tippy-top of a pyramid in Egypt with Rude Alf.

BRAINLESS BRIAN

BRIAN likes to think of himself as a quiet dinosaur who enjoys time alone on the beach, listening to classical music. But everyone else sees him as a loud dino stomping around and looking menacing.

EXTINCT EDDIE

EDDIE is ALWAYS hungry. He eats ten meals a day: Two breakfasts, two lunches, two dinners, two snacks, and two desserts. At least he does the dishes.

LUNATIC LEXI

LEXI loves to carb up while bingeing on her latest sci–fi obsession. Pasta, breadsticks, bagels, garlic knots . . . She'll stuff her puppy face while speeding through novels set in an alien galaxy. But when it's time to curl up in her dog bed, watch a movie, and bite her ChewToyBacca, do not disturb her.

BUFORD BUTTSNIFFER

BUFORD has a stinky sense of humor *and* taste. Meaning . . . he eats poo. He can sniff out a fresh doggy bag from sixteen miles away. He occasionally sees Super Doofus flying overhead, and he's pleased whenever Doofus fails at his missions. Buford doesn't like superheroes. You can't save everyone. Optimism is pointless.

DASTARDLY DANIEL

If you're on the hunt for **DASTARDLY DANIEL**, you better be quick. He is one speedy owl. He can fly over 100 miles per hour! And yes, that's above the flight limit. Does Daniel care? No. He'll flap his wings right in your face if you tell him to slow down. Pass him a pizza slice with olives and rats on it, though, and you'll win him over.

DOLLY LLAMA

Anyone who thinks llamas are zenned-out animals has not met **DOLLY LLAMA**. This spunky llama trained in India to be a temporary-tattoo artist and only came back to America to escape the hordes of annoying alpacas. She'll give you the coolest rose tattoo design, but if you stiff her on a tip, be prepared for her mighty launch of . . . spit, spit, spit!

EVIL EDEN

EDEN gets her name from her devilish yet hypnotizing grin. Some call her the Evil Farmer-Charmer, because somehow she can sneak onto farms, eat as much produce as she wants, and leave zero trace evidence.

HENRY WHODUNNIT

If any Feisty Pets are looking for someone to tell them a scary story, they call on **HENRY WHODUNNIT** to snap his beak. And he's not making any of these stories up. His creepy tale about flying around an old castle during a full moon and encountering a rabid werewolf eating breakfast for dinner? True. No one has dared to ask what exactly the werewolf was eating.

ICE COLD IZZY

ICE COLD IZZY is a formal penguin who holds his beak high. When he hits the islands with his bright blue surfboard, all the Feisty Pets on shore know to move aside. The Big Kahuna bird is here to waddle over and make some waves. If Izzy crushes the surf for too long and gets sunburned, watch out for his penguin wrath.

LOUIE LADYKILLER

LOUIE LADYKILLER is on a mission to prove any turtle speed-shamers wrong. He's the fastest Feisty Pet racecar driver around, and can plummet down slopes, snowboarding as fast as an Olympic gold medalist. He and Lightning Bolt Lenny have still not settled their video game feud of '17. They turned their game controllers into weapons. It was brutal.

MARY MONSTERTRUCK

MARY made her own banjo out of a toilet paper roll (that she unrolled) and a tissue box. She started the first Feisty Pets bluegrass band with Vicky Vicious before Vicky decided to go rock-and-roll. Mary has won talent shows for both her banjo AND fiddling skills. Make sure you applaud this kitty when she's onstage, or her claws will come out.

SLY SISSYPANTS

SLY is the Pet you go to if you need to put a plan in motion. What kind of plan? A sneaky plan. He is a fox, after all. Sly's particularly good at causing a diversion and then stealthily going about his business. He's quick on his feet and can slip away unseen from any incriminating scene. Definitely pick him for your laser tag team.

SUZIE SWEARJAR

SUZIE'S only form of exercise is running her mouth. Otherwise, she'd rather just lie back and run the mud tap on the bath. This pig is fond of her "me time." Her favorite way to relax involves bacon to nibble on (What? It's delicious.), therapeutic oils, and some mud suds. But if Suzie hears one note from "Old MacDonald," watch out—the peace is over.

ALI CORNBALL

ALI CORNBALL is the FIRST Feisty Pet of her kind. She's not a unicorn. She's not a Pegasus. She's an alicorn. Don't know what that is? She doesn't care. Ali wants you to know is that she is one-of-a-kind and you better not forget it. Glenda and Sparkles are her gal squad, but they're frenemies at best. Hoof manicures and FlySky spin classes really have to be done in a group.

FEISTY LIFE

TO BE FEISTY, you have to live feisty. The Feisty Pets gang incorporate their notorious mischief into every part of their day-to-day lives! Even during activities like an average drive around the neighborhood or an evening at home cooking dinner, each Pet manages to mix up mundane routines with troublemaking.

To maintain a proper balance of sass and sweetness, follow the feisty way of life!

FEISTY TIPS

FOR A HEALTHY AND HAPPY LIFE

FEED THE FEISTY

MMM. SUGAR.

GOLDEN RULE:
All Feisty Pets know that
the main food group is
CANDY.

If you want a friend to make you a delicious **FEISTY PIE...**

... smile and ask **NICELY.**

But if you **DEMAND** pie, be warned . . .

You'll get a delicious pie, all right . . .

PIE!

Straight to the **FACE.**

DIY HEALTH SMOOTHIE

* 3 c. liquid base
* 2 tbsp. protein powder
* 1-½ c. green beans
* 1 c. fruit
* ½ c. hazelnuts

A healthy Feisty smoothie should consist of all **"natural"** elements.

Smoothies need to have a liquid base. Maple syrup should work fine because of its sticky smooth consistency.

Pixy Stix can be substituted for protein powder.

WHAT? They're powder. And sugar has protein, right?

PROTEIN POWDER

2

Green beans can be the jelly kind.

3

GREEN BEANS

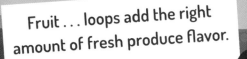

Fruit . . . loops add the right amount of fresh produce flavor.

4

To make it as organic as possible, throw in some gummy worms.

5

WORMS

Even though the recipe calls for hazelnuts, any candy bar with nuts in it is totally fine to add. Chocolate is good for you, honestly.

6

It's so, so healthy!
Let the healing
commence.

**WITH EXTRA
SUGAR!**

This healthy smoothie is
CLEANSING.
It does not stir you into
a sugar spiral at all . . .

GET FIT.

WORK IN SOME

FEISTY

FITNESS

There's totally no judgment at the Feisty Fit & Sweat Center . . .

But if you drop your 1,000-pound dumbbell on your toe while dead-lifting, that's ON YOU!

FITNESS FIRST.

Unless you're tired and want ice cream. That's probably a better idea.

DON'T FORGET
YOUR ANNUAL CHECKUPS

For cats, getting shots during checkups is a necessity.

So? Am I healthy?! That shot hurt, you know.

CURIOSITY

Well, your curiosity levels are high. If we don't get these down, they could kill you!

Dogs need to take a nose exam at least twice a year.

Once a dog is presented with butt samples, the sniff testing can begin.

Golden Doodle!

Bassett Hound!

Tabby cat!

BUTT SAMPLES:
- ☒ **Golden Doodle**
- ☑ **Basset Hound**
- ☐ **Tabby Cat**

I like sniffing butts.

Well, Sammy, that is one top-of-the-line sniffer! Your nose is healthy as can be.

GET CRAFTY

Has your phone been smashed too many times because you practice martial arts in abandoned parking lots?

The Feisty Pets suggest you make your own phone case! Don't be afraid to customize it like crazy. Now it looks like a friend.

Some Pets **DESPERATELY** need one.

Then you can have fun asking your new phone friend to tell you a joke!

Tell me a joke, you hidden phone robot who knows everything!

This is a joke

Phones are feisty, too. They can turn on you any second.

DANCE IT OUT

Go for a joy ride with your best friend and blast the hottest hit songs.

And if your jam comes on, just bust a move, right then and there!

Feistyyyy, don't you loveee meee!

I'm loving your dance moves, AND you're causing a traffic jam!

Sightseeing around the world with friends is so much fun . . . But it doesn't count unless everyone sees how much fun you're having on social media.

TRAVEL

Gotta take that pic for Petstagram.

Oh, and that goofy selfie for SnapPet. #NoFeistyFilter

PARTY TIME
WITH THE FEISTY PETS

Birthday parties are the perfect place to show off your best hats.

Just be careful with your hat at a dragon's birthday party.

Who thought it was a good idea to let a dragon blow out candles?

Need a party trick in a pinch?
Ceiling fans work perfectly.

Everyone can hop on and spin,
just as the DJ spins tracks.

When the crew is getting too rowdy . . . just **BOUNCE.**

TRAMPOLINE style.

53

HOLIDAYS
WITH THE FEISTY PETS

Halloween is really nothing special for the Feisty Pets, since they dress up on a daily basis and always have full access to candy, stolen or not . . .

HALLOWEEN

But Katy Cobweb uses Halloween as her day to let the other Pets know not to cross her.

You know you're cursed, right, Katy? My sister told me not to come to your Halloween party because you're bad luck.

Oh, thanks for telling me, Sammy.

I'll just make sure her Halloween party doesn't happen at all.

Too cool for a Christmas tree? No problem.

The holiday is all about the shiny lights anyway.

Just grab some Christmas lights off a decorated tree no one is using, and deck out a festive friend instead.

INSTANT
jolly decoration.

You could even say he glows!

PETS' GUIDE TO FEISTY FUROCIOUS FUN!

TO ENJOY A STRESS-FREE LIFE, get on board with the Feisty Pets' motto: Have fun first, worry later. Or, actually, don't worry at all— just stick your tongue out and move on. From Cuddles Von Rumblestrut's passion for cliff diving to Vicky Viscious's habit of chewing electrical cords, the Feisty gang are all for reckless activities.

Here's how to incorporate FUN, EX-CITEMENT, and DANGER into your daily life in just the right *feisty* way.

HOBBIES!

ACTIVITIES! SAFETY HAZARDS!

If someone steals your **CANDY,** challenge them to a casual drone race through the forest.

Drone racing is not only **DANGEROUS,** it's liberating!

And if your opponent crash-lands . . .

What a perfect opportunity to make s'mores!

Ooey, gooey
VICTORY.

Bubble wrap provides endless satisfying fun!

POP, POP, POP . . .

Actually, when all the bubbles are popped, the fun does end.

It's
DEVASTATING.

SPORTS
WITH THE PETS

Game day viewing parties can be awesome ragers when rivals root for their sides to win.

Get decked out in your game gear, grab your feistiest flags, and cheer, cheer, cheer!

Spoiler alert: the Polar Bears always win against the Seals.

So make sure you provide enough meaty and spicy snacks to keep any Pets from getting a bit too … excited about the win.

KARATE CHOP

Any karate master knows that karate chopping is the way to glory. You can karate chop anything! Use what you have around you, like pencils . . .

Sewing thread towers . . .

Even plastic cup towers! Honestly, chopping towers is SO advanced.

And when it's time for a challenge?

PORK CHOP!

SUPER DOOFUS'S GUIDE
TO SAVING FRIENDS AND IMPRESSING PEOPL

1. Have a super-slick disguise and use an inventive changing room.

2. Your costume shows the world you are a hero. Capes are awesome.

3. Determine your superhero power and show it off. Flying is the BEST!

4. Try not to make mistakes. *See note.

Businessman by day . . .

Super Doofus by night! Or also during the day! Or in the morning, too, if a Feisty Pet needs me . . .

SUPER DOOFUS!

Dropping the Pet you just saved from high in the air.

Or, dropping yourself too suddenly . . .

. . . from high in the air.

THE FEISTY ARTS

PHOTOGRAPHY

Selfie-taking can be a blast and an ego boost. Don't forget to show your chompers and smile with your eyes!

Just hope that a slasher wielding an axe who is sneaking up behind you doesn't ruin it.

DRAWING

Drawing is a great form of creative expression. Use a friend as your muse!

DUH!

Draw from the soul and be true to your subject . . . even if they look **DOOFY.** 🐾

73

VICKY VICIOUS'S RULES
FOR ROCKING OUT

Feeling stressed? Rock out your rage, **RABBIT** style!

1. Master every instrument. Who needs band members when you got yourself? They'll probably mess everything up anyway.

2. Pick a sweet band name, like *Bun*illa Ice.

3. "Bohemian *rabbit*-sody" is the most important and easiest song to cover.

4. Come up with a signature expression when you riff hard or pound the drums. You'll look WAY cooler.

FEISTY FRIENDS AND... ENEMIES

AS ANY FEISTY PET KNOWS,

when you're a little bit sweet and a lot bit sassy, friends can turn to enemies at the drop of a sparkly top hat. But pranks and major attitude problems spice up any friendship!

Who wants a boring trip to the mall without passing any judgment on your friends' clothing choices in the store?

DON'T BE RUDE...
BE FEISTY

Chickens!

Don't call your Feisty friends chickens! It's rude.

Unless they're . . . you know, actual chickens.

Like . . . your-phone-deserves-a-bat-to-the-screen rude.

Now, what was I saying?

Jacuzzi time with friends is relaxing.

Until they fart.
EW.

It wasn't me!

Unless you like smelly farts!

I like sniffing butts.

BEING A TRUE
FEISTY FRIEND

If you're the third wheel on an outing with your friends who are a couple, and they get into a fight—especially a fiery one, like Ferdinand Flamefart and Sparkles Rainbowbarf tend to have . . .

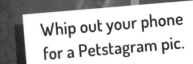

Whip out your phone for a Petstagram pic.

Fixes
EVERYTHING!

Now all is back
to sweetness.
PERFECT!

Or not . . .

At least they looked
cute on Petstagram.

FEISTY FRIEND ADVICE

Feisty Friends are always there to provide you with advice when you need it.

Hey, Bobby, how do you like my skirt?

But it may not be exactly what you want to hear . . .

I present you with the seal of approval!

And that skirt STINKS!

TREND-SETTING, THE FEISTY WAY

BEING TRENDY COMES NATURALLY to the Feisty Pets. From their stylish outfits to their knowledge of everything viral on the internet, they are true trendsetters. If you want to know the latest video influencer, tune into Glenda Glitterpoop's vlogs. Need some updates on music? Sammy Suckerpunch and Princess Pottymouth are always riffing on the sickest jams out there to stream.

The Feisty Pets are on the social media prowl and you better be keeping up. Or you'll be one basic ball of fluff.

JAMMING OUT
WITH THE FEISTY GANG

If you're onstage, put on a show like the true performer you are! Stay confident, but beware . . . crowds can turn on you.

It's me and you, in the Feisty crew! So get ready to watch me move.

GIVE ME A BEAT!

AHHH! Not a *beet!*

Yep, Feisty crowds do **EXACTLY** what they're told . . .

THE FEISTY PETS
TEACH YOU TO PRODUCE DOPE MUSIC VIDEOS

Cats vs. Dogs Rap Battles are the feistiest trend in hip-hop music right now.

But more and more Pets are starting to get into the music video game.

SAMMY SUCKERPUNCH'S rules for rad dog rap videos:

1. Wear bad-to-the-bone sunglasses.
2. Incorporate flying money.
3. Don't forget those sick chains.
4. Rely on your homedogs to back you up.

PRINCESS POTTYMOUTH'S rules for cool cat rap videos:

1. Wear pretty kitty sunglasses.
2. Digital fire backgrounds are a must-have (actual flame on fur is NOT cute)
3. Feature a hot car.
4. Make it shiny. And sassy.

GLENDA GLITTERPOOP'S rules for slaying rap videos:

1. Bathe in a tub of jewels and diamonds.
2. Feature other icons like MC Marky Mischief.
3. Shaking your tail is the most important choreography in your arsenal.
4. Mix up your fashion throughout every scene. We're talking fur shrugs, patterned hoodies, sequined tops, tiaras . . . glitz it up!

GLENDA GLITTERPOOP'S GUIDE

TO WHAT SHINES AND WHAT STINKS

Daily vlogging? **SHINES.**

Turning into a giant and wreaking havoc on a city? **STINKS.**

Crafting DIY projects while wearing a fashionable choker? **SHINES.**

Unboxing a tiny version of yourself? **STINKS!**

Who is this mini impostor?

She looks GLITTERPOOPY-GORGEOUS!

Giving makeup tutorials? **SHINES.**

95

Now that you know the basic rules to be the feistiest you can be, feel free to flash a fierce smile and tear away any pages in this guide that you like. The main thing to know is that rules are made to be broken. As long as you're having fun, it's okay to

The only rule is to sniff butts.

It's best to poop on rule books.

Actually, I make the rules.